Idea #10,473
SKWID

(Scientific Kinetic Waterproof Investigation Device)

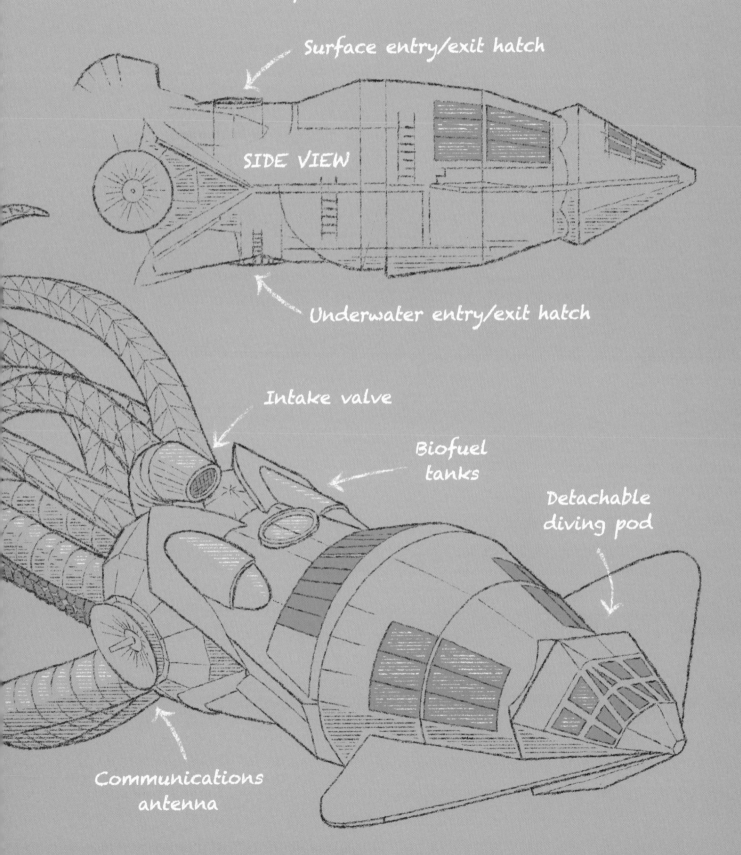

Surface entry/exit hatch

SIDE VIEW

Underwater entry/exit hatch

Intake valve

Biofuel tanks

Detachable diving pod

Communications antenna

MAD SCIENTIST
ACADEMY

THE OCEAN DISASTER

MATTHEW McELLIGOTT

CROWN BOOKS
FOR YOUNG READERS
NEW YORK

To Christy, and to Jean, an exceptional teacher, mentor, designer, and friend

ACKNOWLEDGMENTS
An ocean of thanks to Dr. Paul Webb, professor of biology at
Roger Williams University, for all his advice and guidance

Copyright © 2019 by Matthew McElligott

All rights reserved. Published in the United States by Crown Books for Young Readers,
an imprint of Random House Children's Books,
a division of Penguin Random House LLC, New York.

Crown and the colophon are registered trademarks of Penguin Random House LLC.

Visit us on the Web! rhcbooks.com

Educators and librarians, for a variety of teaching tools,
visit us at RHTeachersLibrarians.com

Library of Congress Cataloging-in-Publication Data
Names: McElligott, Matthew, author.
Title: The ocean disaster / Matthew McElligott.
Description: First edition. | New York : Crown Books for Young Readers, [2019] | Series: Mad scientist academy | Audience: Age 5–8. |
Audience: K to Grade 3. | Summary: Dr. Cosmic's class of clever monsters explore the dark depths of the ocean
in the fourth book of the Mad Scientist Academy series. —Provided by publisher.
Identifiers: LCCN 2018052812 | ISBN 978-1-5247-6719-8 (trade) | ISBN 978-1-5247-6720-4 (lib. bdg.) | ISBN 978-1-5247-6721-1 (ebook)
Subjects: LCSH: Marine biology—Juvenile literature. | Marine animals—Juvenile literature. | BISAC: JUVENILE FICTION / Action &
Adventure / General. | JUVENILE FICTION / School & Education. | JUVENILE FICTION / Science & Technology.
Classification: LCC QH91.16 .M44 2019 | DDC 577.7—dc23

The text of this book is set in Sunshine.
The illustrations were created with ink, pencil, and digital techniques.

MANUFACTURED IN CHINA
10 9 8 7 6 5 4 3 2 1
First Edition

When we reach the reef, I'll need to prepare the pod. While I do, Professor Fathom will take you outside for today's lesson.

But we're underwater! How will we breathe?

Don't worry! You'll use these air tanks.

Why only four tanks?

Great question, Ken! Almost all creatures need oxygen to survive...

Not robots!

...and most of us get oxygen by breathing air with our lungs. Some, like fish, get oxygen from water, using gills.

However, Professor Fathom and Tad are amphibious. That means they can do both.

No fair!

We'll use these special microphones so we can talk with the rest of you.

Grab your handbooks and let's go for a swim!

It's a bunch of tiny creatures. They're eating something even smaller.

The handbook says they're called plankton.

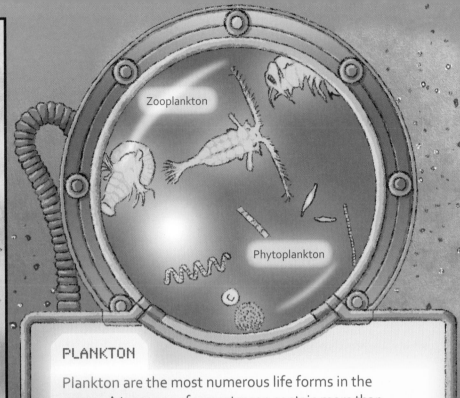

Zooplankton

Phytoplankton

PLANKTON

Plankton are the most numerous life forms in the ocean. A teaspoon of seawater can contain more than a million organisms.

PHYTOPLANKTON

- Smallest producers
- Get their energy from the sun
- Are the base of the ocean food web

ZOOPLANKTON

- Smallest consumers
- Eat phytoplankton
- Include tiny animals such as krill, fish larvae (baby fish), and copepods

Everyone! Thora and I solved the puzzle. It's plankton!

Great job, you two!

WOOOOOOOOOOOOOOOOOO

Hey, Tad, do you hear that?

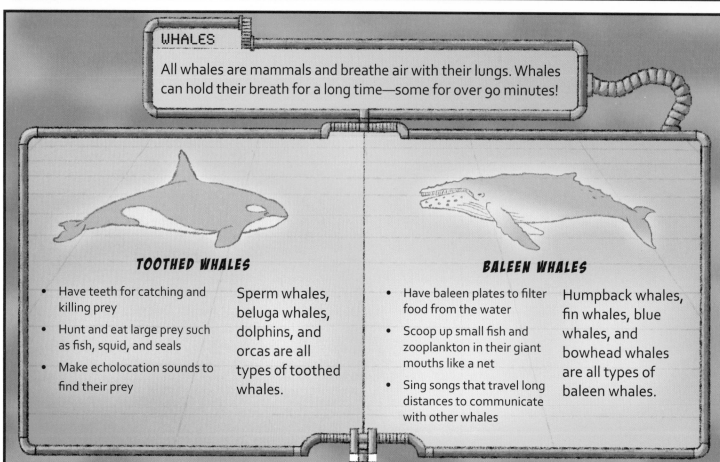

WHALES

All whales are mammals and breathe air with their lungs. Whales can hold their breath for a long time—some for over 90 minutes!

TOOTHED WHALES

- Have teeth for catching and killing prey
- Hunt and eat large prey such as fish, squid, and seals
- Make echolocation sounds to find their prey

Sperm whales, beluga whales, dolphins, and orcas are all types of toothed whales.

BALEEN WHALES

- Have baleen plates to filter food from the water
- Scoop up small fish and zooplankton in their giant mouths like a net
- Sing songs that travel long distances to communicate with other whales

Humpback whales, fin whales, blue whales, and bowhead whales are all types of baleen whales.

Enjoy the ride, students! See you soon!

Soon...

Look! Rays!

Dolphins!

THUNK!

What was that?

We're slowing down!

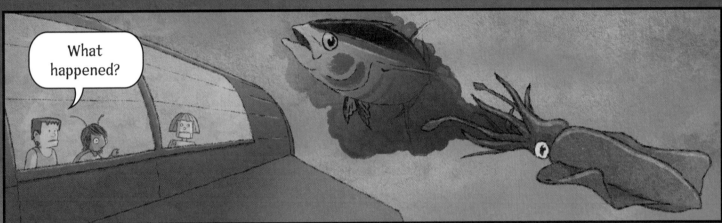

The handbook says squid defend themselves by shooting out a cloud of dark ink.

SQUID

HEARTS
All squid have three hearts.

EYES
The giant squid has the largest eyes of any animal.

SIPHON
A water jet used to move the squid and squirt ink.

INK
Squid defend themselves by squirting a dark, ink-like fluid into the water to confuse attackers.

ARMS & TENTACLES
Squid have eight arms and two tentacles with suction cups for catching prey.

SIZES
There are more than 300 types of squid. The smallest is less than one inch long (one cm), about the size of your thumbnail.

The longest is up to 43 feet (13 m), almost as long as a school bus!

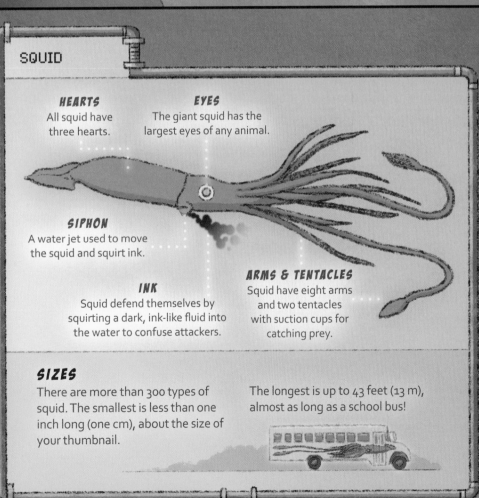

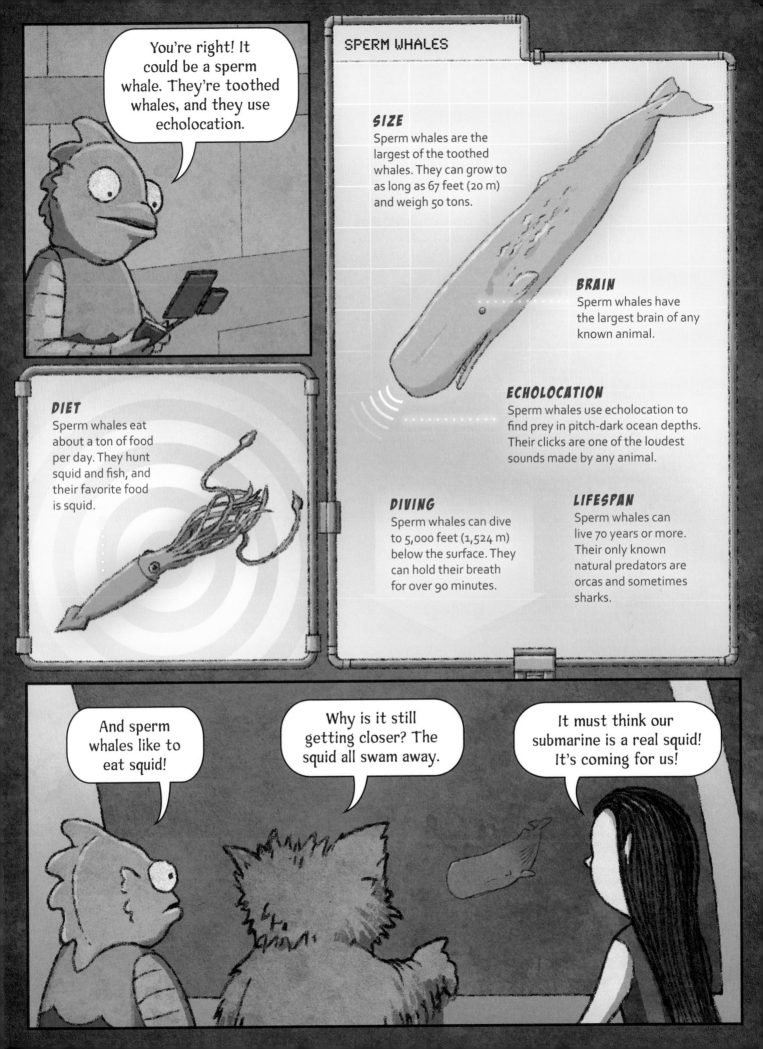

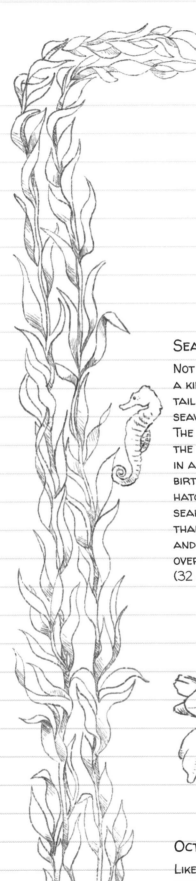

Giant Kelp

The largest seaweed at over 100 feet (30 m) long. Kelp can grow up to 2 feet (0.6 m) per day!

Dr. Cosmic,
Here are some amazing ocean organisms for your students to look for on future sea expeditions.

—Professor Fathom

Emperor Penguin

The largest penguin at 4 feet (1.2 m) tall. An emperor has a thick layer of fat and specialized feathers, which help keep it warm even during −40°F (−40°C) winters in Antarctica.

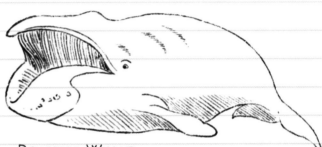

Seahorse

Not a horse, but a kind of fish. Its tail can hold on to seaweed or coral. The male carries the female's eggs in a pouch and gives birth when they hatch. The smallest seahorse is less than 1/2 inch (1.1 cm) and the largest is over 1 foot long (32 cm).

Bowhead Whale

Lives in the Arctic Ocean. Bowheads have a life span of more than 200 years, making them the longest-living mammal on Earth. They can grow up to 59 feet (18 m) long.

Sea Turtle

One of the few kinds of reptiles that live in the ocean. The largest, the leatherback, can grow to over 2,000 pounds (907 kg). A leatherback travels 10,000 miles (16,100 km) or more in a year.

For more ocean facts, links, projects, and games, be sure to visit madscientistacademybooks.com

Octopus

Like squid, octopuses are invertebrates (they don't have a spine). The common octopus can change the color and pattern of its skin to hide in plain sight on the seafloor.

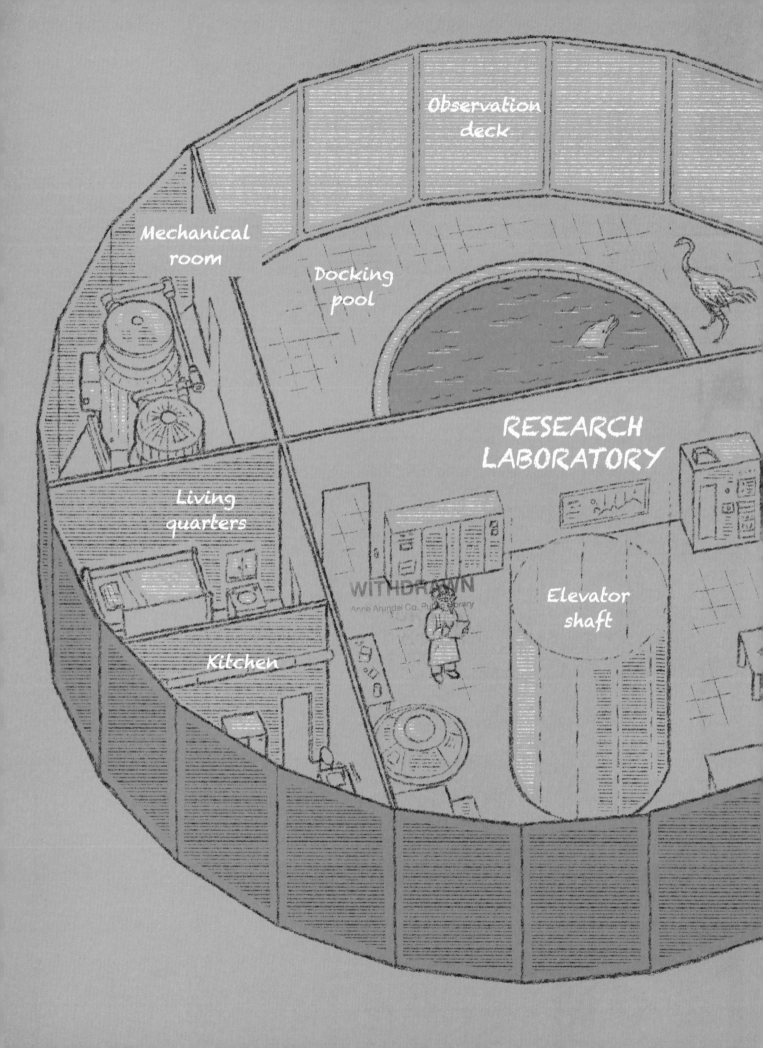

Observation deck

Mechanical room

Docking pool

RESEARCH LABORATORY

Living quarters

Elevator shaft

Kitchen